First
Shapes

Educational Consultant: Betty Root

Betty Root has a lifetime of experience in education, as a teacher, lecturer and consultant. She has written, or acted as advisor on, numerous books for primary and pre-school children.

First published in Great Britain in 2000 by Egmont UK Limited
This edition published in 2010 by Dean, an imprint of Egmont UK Limited
239 Kensington High Street, London, W8 6SA

Based on the 'Winnie-the-Pooh' works by A.A. Milne and E.H. Shephard.
© 2010 Disney Enterprises, Inc.
All rights reserved.

ISBN 978 0 6035 6271 6

7 9 10 8 6
Printed in Italy

All rights reserved. No part of this publication may be reproduced, stored in a retrieval system, or transmitted, in any form or by any means, electronic, mechanical, photocopying, recording or otherwise, without the prior permission of the publisher and copyright owner.

Here are Winnie-the-Pooh and his friends,
with the shapes you will find in this book.

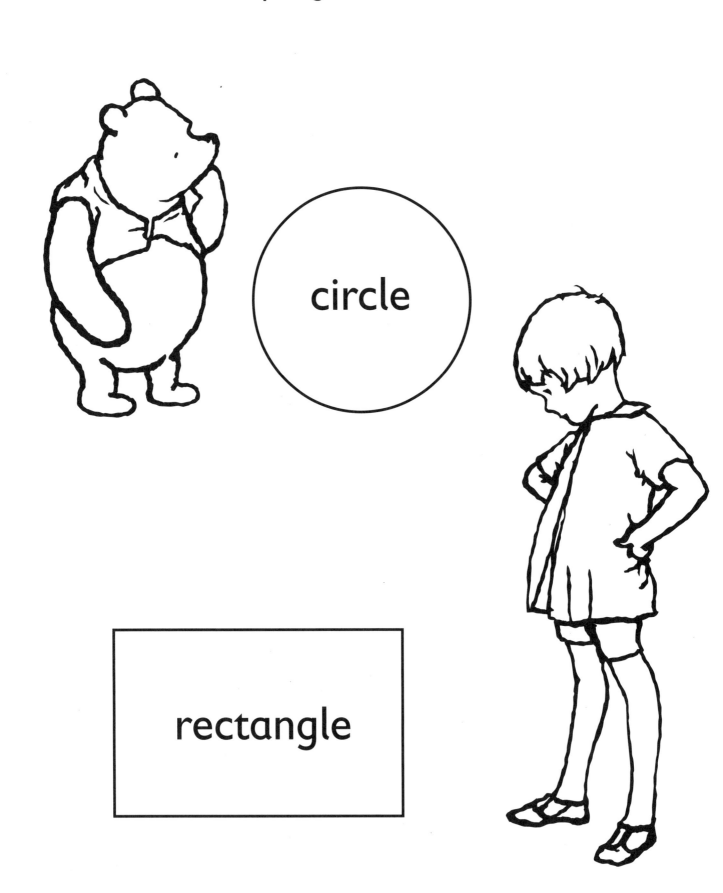

circle

rectangle

Pooh's favourite shape is a circle. Christopher Robin's favourite shape is a rectangle. Piglet's favourite shape is a triangle and Eeyore's favourite shape is a square. Which is your favourite shape?

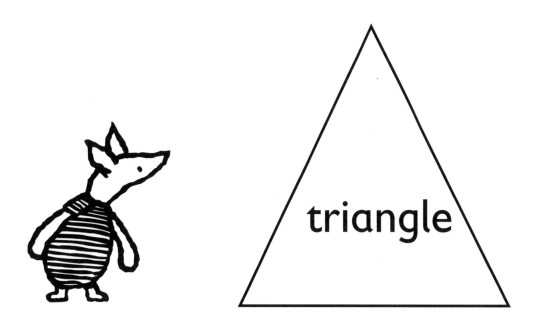

circle ⭕

Trace over a circle with your finger. Starting with your pencil on the big dot, draw over the dotted lines. Then, draw some circles of your own.

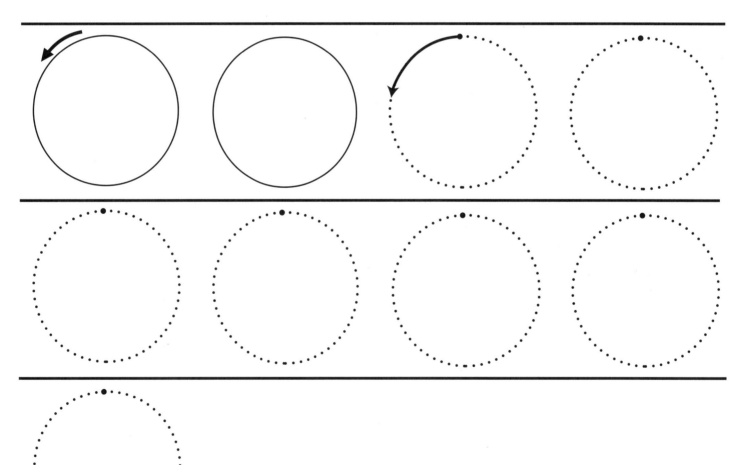

square □

Trace over a square
with your finger.
Starting with your pencil
on the big dot, draw
over the dotted lines.
Then, draw some
squares of your own.

triangle △

Trace over a triangle
with your finger.
Starting with your pencil
on the big dot, draw
over the dotted lines.
Then, draw some
triangles of your own.

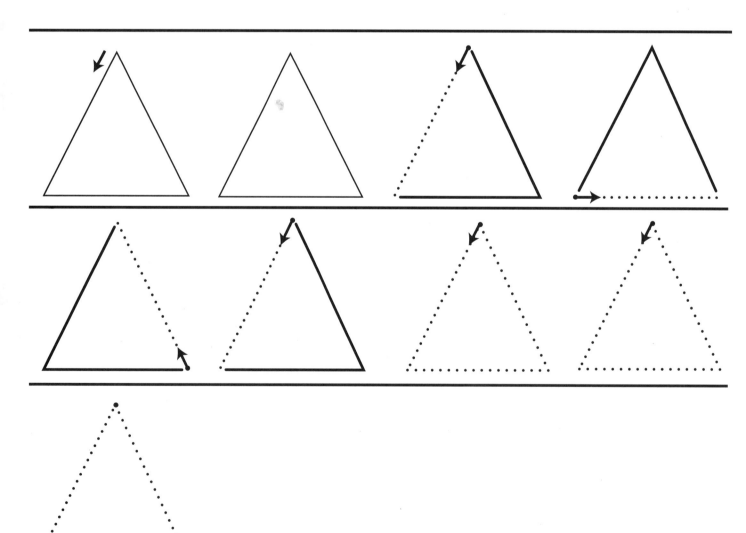

rectangle ▭

Trace over a rectangle
with your finger.
Starting with your pencil
on the big dot, draw
over the dotted lines.
Then, draw some
rectangles of your own.

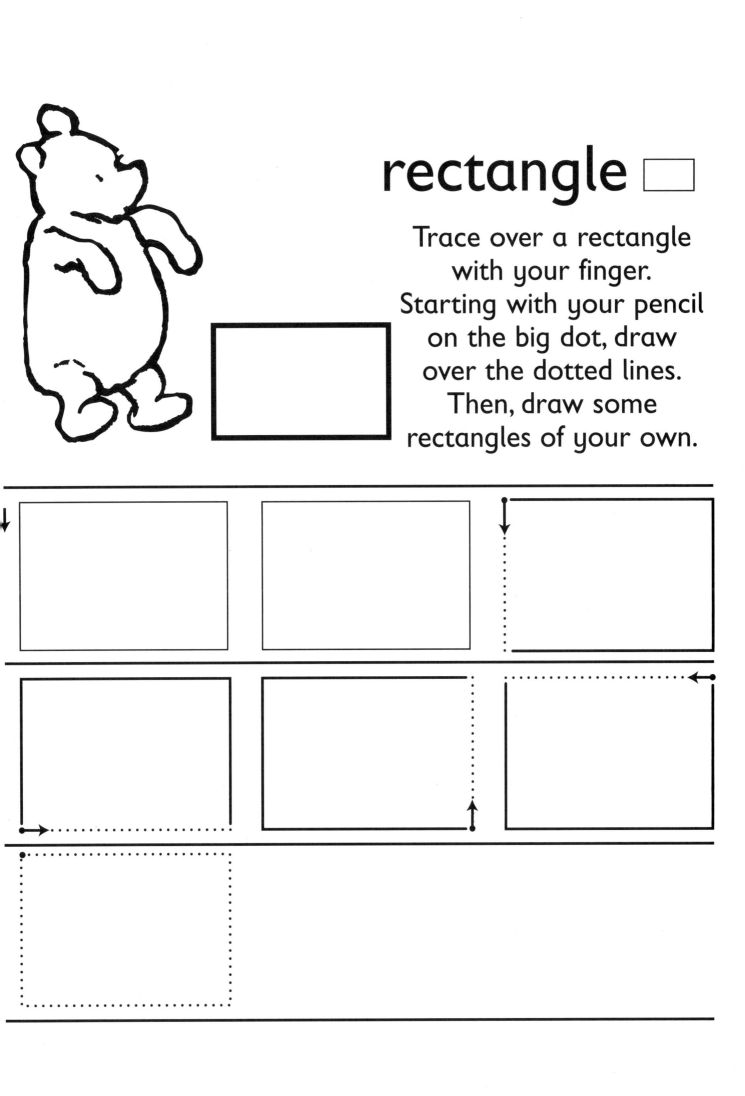

Match the shapes that are the same.

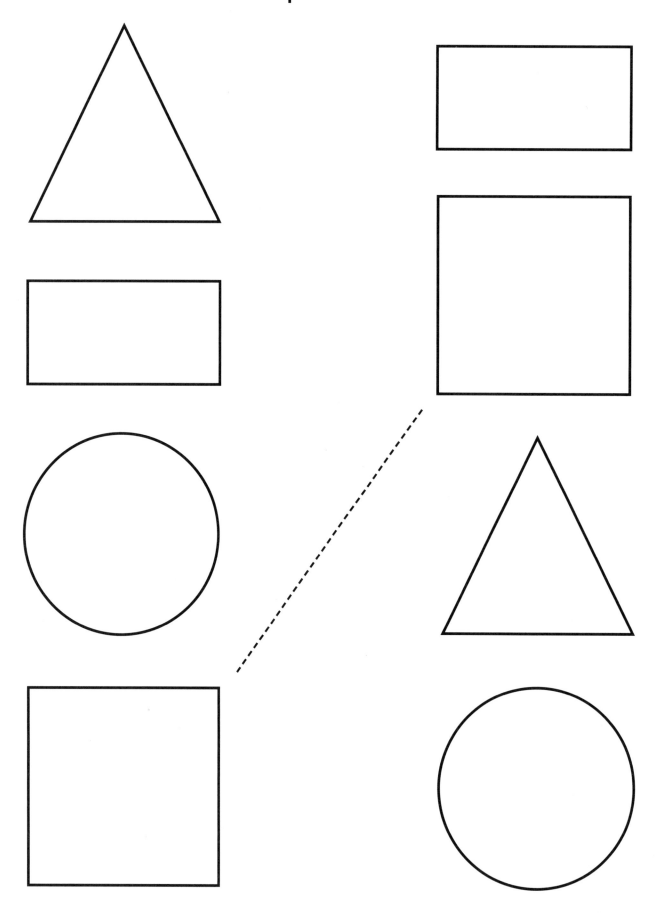

Christopher Robin is looking for his friends. Can you help him find them? Follow the shapes.

Colour the odd one out in each row.

Find all these shapes in the picture and colour them in.

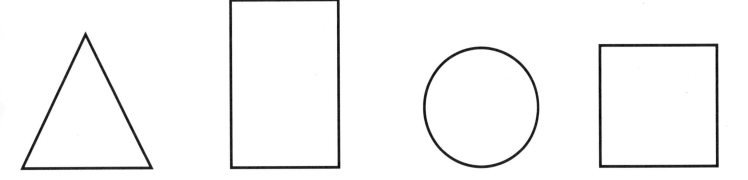

Rabbit wants you to draw the shapes
with him. Trace over the dotted lines.

Match the shapes that are the same.

Draw the shape that comes next in each row.

Put a cross through the odd one out in each row.

You can use shapes to make pictures of Pooh and his friends. Here are Pooh, Piglet and Eeyore. Trace over the dotted lines to finish the pictures.

Pooh

Piglet

Eeyore

Here are Christopher Robin, Roo and Rabbit too!
Colour in all the pictures.

Christopher
Robin

Rabbit

Roo

Pooh and his friends are different sizes.
Pooh is big but Small is small.
Put a line through all the ones which
are small. Colour the big ones.

Pooh

Small

Roo

Kanga

Christopher Robin

Piglet

Match the big and small shapes that are the same.

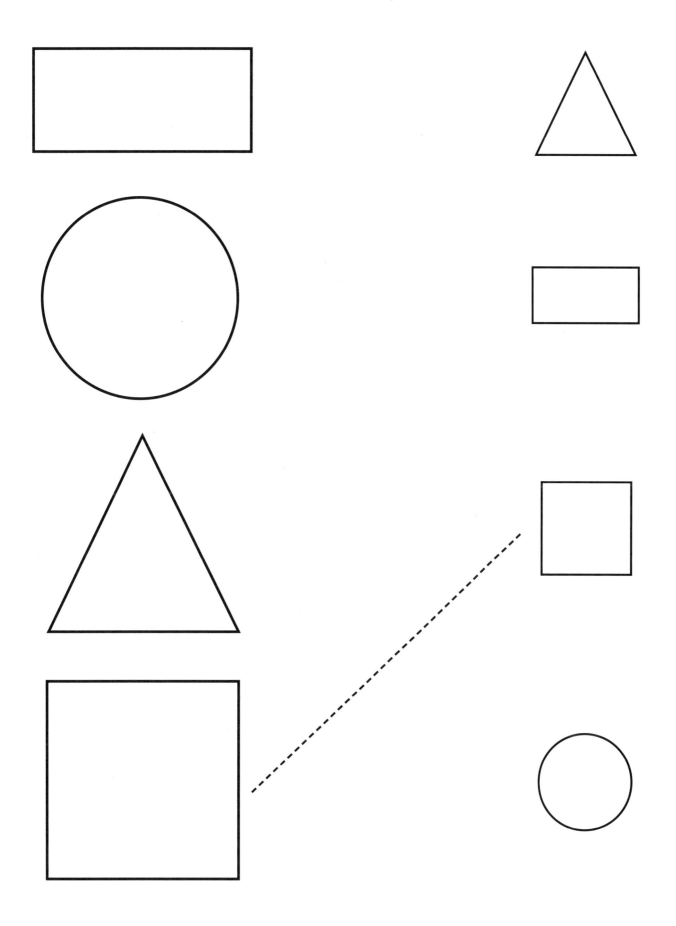

Colour the big picture in each line.

Colour the small shape in each line.

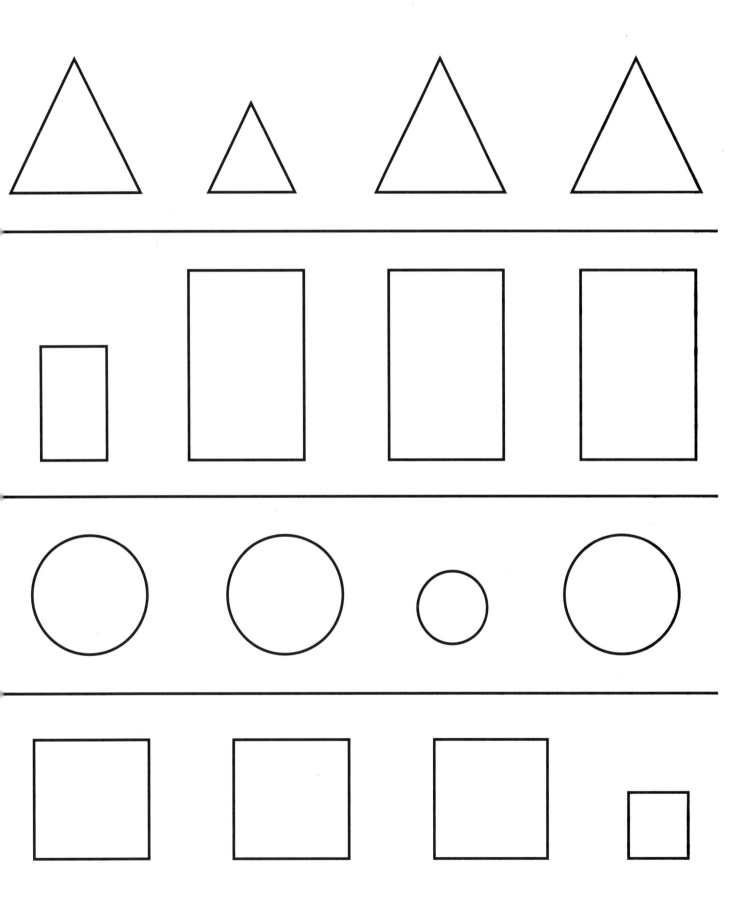

Colour the small picture in each line.

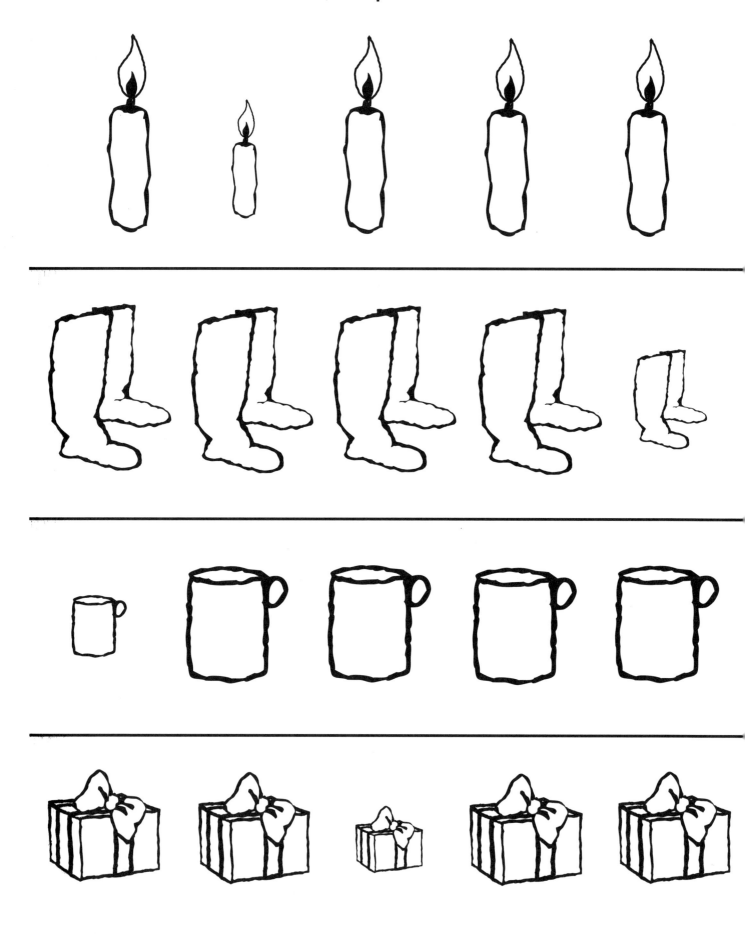

One of Pooh's friends looks very big. Colour him in.

Shapes and Sizes

This book is part of a series designed to prepare children for starting school. The following skills are covered in this book:

• drawing circles, triangles, squares and rectangles
• recognising these shapes as part of a larger picture
• identifying big and small, biggest and smallest

The aim at this stage is to build confidence and make learning as much fun as possible. By working on these activities with your child, you can offer help and encouragement, and share the fun. Here are a few simple ways that you can help your child to get the most out of this book:

• Start at the beginning of the book and work through each page. The activities get gradually more difficult, building on what your child has learnt.

• Short sessions are more likely to hold your child's attention, so do not try to do too much in one go. You might start with just one activity. Stop if your child is losing concentration or an activity seems too difficult - you can always come back to it later.

• Be sure to reward your child's efforts with encouraging words. If your child feels successful, they will be keen to learn next time.

• Discuss each activity with your child to make certain that it is understood before any writing takes place. Asking questions and puzzling out the activities together is an important part of the learning process.

• As your child draws the shapes, saying the names of the shapes is helpful.

• You can help to reinforce what your child has learnt in this book by talking about sizes and recognising shapes when you are out together.

• If your child has never met Winnie-the-Pooh and his friends before, discover their adventures in *Winnie-the-Pooh* and *The House at Pooh Corner*.